A MILE FROM
ELLINGTON STATION

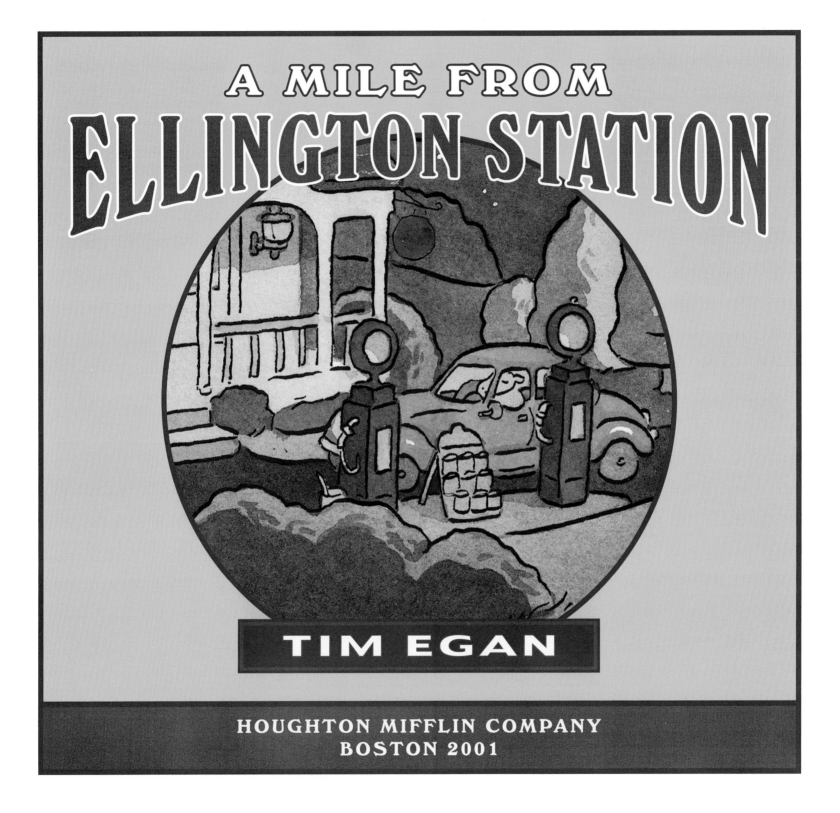

TIM EGAN

HOUGHTON MIFFLIN COMPANY
BOSTON 2001

For Ann, my beautiful wife

www.houghtonmifflinbooks.com

The text of this book is set in 16-point ITC Berkeley Oldstyle.
The illustrations are ink and watercolor on paper.

Library of Congress Cataloging-in-Publication Data

Egan, Tim.
A mile from Ellington station / Tim Egan.
p.   cm.
Summary: Jealous of the highly talented dog Marley,
Preston the bear spreads a rumor that the dog is a wizard.
ISBN 0-618-00393-2
[1. Dogs — Fiction. 2. Bears — Fiction. 3. Animals — Fiction.
4. Jealousy — Fiction.]   I. Title.
PZ7.E2815 Mi 2001
[E] — dc21
00-031897

Manufactured in the United States of America
BVG 10 9 8 7 6 5 4 3 2 1

As the train whistle sounded in the distance, Preston won his nine hundred and forty-third game of checkers in a row. He hadn't lost a game in over a year.

"You're the greatest checkers-playing bear in the world," declared Jacob.

"Yeah," agreed Elwood, "you're like a checkers genius."

Preston took a bow as his wife, Ruth, rolled her eyes.

Ruth and Preston owned Ellington Lodge, which was about a mile from the train station. The lodge had a general store, a couple of gas pumps, and five small cabins. Lately, because Preston was so preoccupied playing checkers, he'd neglected his chores. Ruth was growing a little tired of it.

"Weren't you going to mow the lawn today, dear?" she asked. "It's really long."

"Just a few more games, Ruth," he answered for the hundredth time.

As Preston beat Eleanor Dorsey in game nine hundred and fifty-six, Ruth said, "Maybe we can start painting the place soon, dear. It's looking a little shabby."

Just then, a small dog strolled in and said, "Excuse me. My name is Marley. I'll paint the place in exchange for a stay at your lodge. I learned to paint in France."

Ruth glanced over at Preston, who was lost in his own world. Then she looked at Marley. He seemed like a trustworthy dog.

"Deal," she said.

After Ruth and Preston went to sleep that night, Marley began painting the lodge. He worked with amazing speed and accuracy. In fact, by sunrise, he had finished painting the entire place. It was a remarkable achievement.

The next morning, everyone marveled at what Marley had done.

"It seems impossible," said Preston, "but hey, now I can really focus on my game."

"It's incredible," said Ruth. "Thank you, Marley. Let's celebrate with breakfast!"

"Splendid!" said Marley. "I used to be a chef in Italy. Mind if I whip something up?"

Nobody minded, so Marley prepared his specialty, Eggs Florentine.

The Briggs, from cabin number four, said it was the best meal they'd ever had.

After breakfast, Marley entertained everyone with stories of his travels to faraway lands.

"You sure are one amazing dog," said Preston. "Care to play a little checkers?"

"Why, I haven't played since Australia," declared Marley.

Preston smiled, and the two of them started playing. Four minutes later, Marley made a triple jump that took the last of Preston's checkers in game nine hundred and ninety-two.

"Good game!" shouted Marley. No one else said a word.

Preston was devastated.

Ruth placed her hand on his shoulder and said, "Remember, dear, it's only a game."

It didn't help.

When Marley realized what had happened, he said, "I'm so sorry, Preston. If I'd known about your streak, I wouldn't have beaten you."

This didn't help either.

That evening, as Marley taught everyone how to say "hello" in ten different languages, Preston just sat in the corner. He suddenly found the little dog a bit obnoxious.

The next night, as Marley blew giant bubbles out on the lawn, Preston asked, "Do you notice anything strange about this Marley character? I mean, how could he paint the whole place in one night? He's like a sorcerer or something."

"Oh, stop it, Preston," said Ruth. "You're just upset because he beat you."

"No, that's not it," said Preston. "He just seems like a sorcerer, that's all."

Jacob and Elwood looked concerned.

"He *is* kind of mystical," said Jacob.

"Exactly," said Preston. "Look at him—he's probably sending signals into the future right now."

They all watched intently as the bubbles floated away into the stars.

The following morning, Preston tried convincing others that Marley was a sorcerer.

"That's ridiculous," said Frank.

Just then, Marley came riding in and said, "Good morning! Mind if I check the weather?"

He flipped the switch on the radio. Nothing happened.

"That radio's broken," explained Preston.

Marley tapped the radio with his cane and a voice came on. It said, "Rain likely today," just as thunder exploded outside and it started pouring. He popped out his umbrella and said, "Well, that was bizarre. Have a great day, all!"

As Marley rode out the door, Preston said, "I'm sorry, but that is *not* a normal dog."

Even Frank looked intrigued.

Preston, Jacob, and Elwood started spreading the sorcerer rumor all over town, and because Marley was so amazing, some folks actually seemed to believe it.

One afternoon, Marley walked up to a group gathered outside the store and, without saying a word, made a dove appear out of thin air. Eleanor screamed.

"Just a trick I learned in Brazil," said Marley.

After he left, Jacob said, "We should all be careful. Legend has it that if sorcerers get mad, they can turn you into ice."

There was a collective shiver.

Frightened, Eleanor ran into the store and told Ruth what they all suspected about the little dog.

The following evening, a large crowd was gathered in the store.

"I know it sounds crazy," said Frank, "but what if Marley is a sorcerer?"

"Yeah!" shouted Elwood. "What if he turns us all into ice cubes?"

They all began mumbling among themselves.

"All of this frightens me!" shouted Eleanor, as the crowd grew even louder.

Preston looked troubled.

"Now, now," he said, "maybe he's just a dog. Let's not get all worked up over this."

But it was a little too late for that.

"I say we run him out of town!" shouted Frank, as more angry noises erupted throughout the store. Soon folks were grabbing kitchen utensils from the wall and marching out the door. Preston was in a panic.

"Enough!" he yelled. "Everyone settle down! I made it up! I admit it! He's not a sorcerer! He's just a small dog with an attitude!"

But by now there was no calming them.

Preston continued pleading, to no avail, as the crowd charged across the lawn toward Marley's cabin. But when they got there, they all stopped suddenly. There, on the porch of the cabin, was Marley, frozen solid.

Ruth came running out of the cabin. "Oh, Preston," she cried, "Marley said if anyone found out he was a sorcerer, he'd turn into ice. And then he did, right in front of me."

Preston couldn't even speak.

"Wow," said Jacob, "I guess I heard the legend wrong."

"What have we done?" asked Elwood.

"He didn't mean us any harm," said Ruth, starting to cry. "He was such a nice dog."

"I can't believe this," said Preston. "I just made all that stuff up. I had no idea. I didn't even believe in sorcerers. But even if he was one, I still liked the little guy. I feel terrible. I'm in shock. I think I'm going to faint."

After a moment, Ruth's sobs turned into soft laughter. Soon Eleanor started laughing as well, and before long, the crowd was in complete hysterics.

Except for Preston, Jacob, and Elwood.

"He's not a sorcerer, you big oafs!" yelled Ruth. "I convinced everyone how absurd it all was, and then we decided to have a little fun with you."

Marley stuck his head out the window and said, "Actually, I'm a Scottish terrier."

Preston looked at the ice statue.

"I learned ice sculpting in Finland!" announced Marley.

Though embarrassed, Preston, Jacob, and Elwood laughed along with everyone else, and they were glad that Marley hadn't turned to ice.

After the necessary apologies were made, Preston mowed the lawn and they all celebrated with another delicious feast, which they insisted Marley prepare.

During dessert, Preston challenged Marley to a rematch in checkers. Marley won the first three games, but then Preston won twelve in a row.

"Ha haa!" he shouted. "Looks like the start of another streak!"

Ruth just smiled and shook her head.